Help! Fwitz lost his Bone

WRITTEN BY: DEANNA M. LOTZ

ILLUSTRATED BY : CHERRY DC

This book is dedicated to:

My Family

143

Mark and Elise

Our Fur babies

Diesel and Quin

Mommy, Sally, Grace and Wilbo

Leia and Lee Lee

Mom

Thanks for introducing us to the Berners.

Take care of our Bella, All of my Love

Until we meet again

Dad

as a token of gratitude and love. Thanks for always being our rock.

Fwitz is a young pup who is full of energy and very playful. He has a wooden box full of his very loved and torn apart toys.

Each morning and throughout the day Fwitz pulls his toys one by one and drops them all over the living room, couch and even brings them outside to his yard. Each night his owner picks his toys up and puts them back into his toy box.

Fwitz seems to favor his
bone most of all.

He annoys his friends with it. He is so clumsy he has dropped his bone many times on Grace's head.

Sometimes he gets so excited he doesn't even notice the cats and he has flopped down on top of Sally and Grace.

Fwitz also lives with Quin. Sometimes she steals his bone for herself!

Fwitz woke up this morning
and went to his toy box.

His bone was not there!? Fwitz searched inside and searched outside!

He began to suspect Quin, Grace, Mommy Cat and Sally.

He thought – Maybe the cats hid it under the couch?

Maybe Quin hid it outside?

Fwitz was so tired from searching that he fell asleep. He started to dream about his favorite bone. His legs started kicking and his nose starting twitching. His dream felt so real he woke himself up!

When Fwitz opened his eyes, he could see his bone inches away from his nose! It was wedged in the corner of the room.

Fwitz happily leaped up to greet his prized bone! He was not sure how it got there.

That did not matter anymore. Fwitz found his bone!